CAMP ROCK

SECOND SESSION #5

Rock Royalty

Rock Royalty

By Lucy Ruggles

Based on "Camp Rock," Written by Karin Gist & Regina Hicks and Julie Brown & Paul Brown

DISNEP PRESS

New York

Printed in the United States of America

First Edition
1 3 5 7 9 10 8 6 4 2

Library of Congress Catalog Card Number: 2008906224
ISBN 978-1-4231-1775-9

For more Disney Press fun, visit www.disneybooks.com
Visit DisneyChannel.com

CHAPTER ONE

The sun was high over Camp Rock, and stomachs were growling. After a full morning of dance practice, voice lessons, and swimming, Mitchie Torres was famished. She couldn't wait to see what her mom, Camp Rock's chef-in-residence, had whipped up for lunch. Normally, Mitchie would have had to help her in the kitchen, but today Connie Torres had given her daughter the day off.

"After all the parties I've had to cater this summer, I think I can handle a little old lunch on my own for once!" Mitchie's mom had assured her, practically pushing Mitchie out the kitchen door that morning.

Now, walking with Lola Scott, Peggy Dupree, and her best friend, Caitlyn Gellar, Mitchie clutched dramatically at her stomach. "Who knew hip-hop could take so much out of a girl!" she cried.

"Yeah," agreed Peggy. "That new move Shane's teaching us—the Crush—is killing me. I just can't seem to get it down."

"Speaking of crushes," said Lola, raising a mischievous eyebrow, "I think someone at Camp Rock might have one on Caitlyn."

Caitlyn's mouth fell open. She blushed as Mitchie, Lola, and Peggy began to giggle. Lola's observation wasn't a surprise to the friends. It had become obvious that a certain camper who had come to Camp Rock for Second Session had taken a special interest not just in the music Caitlyn liked to produce on her laptop, but in the producer herself.

Caitlyn immediately sputtered out a protest. "Mac does *not* have a crush on me!"

"I didn't mention Mac." Lola grinned. "You did."

Caitlyn turned a deeper shade of magenta, and the other girls laughed harder.

Mac Wilson was Colby Miller's bunkmate. The two newbies had become friends even though they were wildly different. Colby was a preppy New Englander while Mac was a Southern boy who played guitar, always quick with a smile and a greeting. Mac was one of those people who got along with everyone—especially Caitlyn.

"Well, I think he's cute," Mitchie said, coming to Caitlyn's aid. "His drawl is adorable."

"What's wrong with meeting someone a little extraspecial at camp?" Peggy shrugged. "It worked for Mitchie."

Now it was Mitchie's turn to turn bright red. It was true that Mitchie and Shane Gray, lead singer of the hot band Connect Three and current Camp Rock guest instructor, had formed a special friendship over the summer. Despite his bad-boy reputation and rock-star attitude upon first arriving at camp, Shane was actually really cool. He and Mitchie just *got* each other. Mitchie had helped Shane get back to his own sound, and he had helped her find her confidence onstage. Still, their friendship was a subject that made Mitchie shy.

Caitlyn laughed and threw her arm around her friend's shoulders. Just as she was about to say something else, the deafening sound of a propeller drowned her out. The wind whipped around them, blowing Mitchie's long brown hair in her face. All at once, every camper walking toward the Mess Hall of Fame turned his or her face to the sky.

It was a helicopter—and it was heading right for Camp Rock!

4

Soon, more campers spilled out of the B-Note canteen in the mess hall's basement and down the paths from the cabins. Everyone wanted to see whose chopper was descending on Camp Rock's front lawn. As the huge aircraft touched down on the grass, they stood with their mouths hanging open.

A moment later, pop sensation T.J. Tyler stepped out of the helicopter.

The star shook her long blond hair out of her face and scanned the growing crowd. T.J. had some exciting news for her daughter Tess, a camper at Camp Rock. She'd decided a surprise visit was in order so she could tell Tess in person.

Besides being an award-winning, multiplatinum recording artist, T.J. Tyler was also the face of Blush Cosmetics. Blush had decided to sponsor a special concert to raise money for after-school music programs. And they wanted their spokesmodel to perform. Knowing how much Tess had enjoyed the music education she'd gotten this summer at Camp Rock, T.J. was more than happy to help.

"Mom!" Tess cried, breaking through the circle of campers and rushing up to her as T.J. came down the helicopter stairs.

"Hi, babe," T.J. said as they air-kissed each other on both cheeks. "I'm on my way to a photo shoot for Blush, but I just heard from Ginger and had to stop by to tell you—"

"Tell me what?!" Tess interrupted, her blue eyes wide. What was so important that her mom had interrupted her busy schedule and come all the way to Camp Rock? It had to be huge!

T.J. smiled. She knew her daughter got her impatient streak from her. "Blush is sponsoring School Rocks, a concert to raise money for after-school music programs. . . ."

"Oh." Tess's face deflated. Just another fund-raiser that would take up her mom's time.

"... *and* they want you and me to perform—together," T.J. continued, beaming.

"Me?" Tess repeated, her eyes growing large. A *sponsored* concert? She would be a household name before the program was even over!

Ella Pador and Lorraine Burgess, Tess's entourage and best friends, had rushed to her side when they saw the helicopter. Now they started jumping up and down, clapping.

"You're gonna be famous!" Ella squealed.

"O.M.G.," gushed Lorraine. "This is so awesome!"

"I'll take that as a yes?" T.J. grinned.

Tess nodded her head enthusiastically. "Yes!" she screamed. Then, composing herself, she added casually, "I'll do it," as if she were agreeing to do the dishes, not sing in a major concert.

"Wonderful," said a happy T.J. "I'll let Ginger know. Now I have to jet, babe. Annie's waiting at the photo studio, and she *hates*

when the talent's late. I'll call you about the details later."

T.J. and Tess double air-kissed again, and just as quickly as she had appeared, T.J. was gone.

CHAPTER TWO

By dinner that night, everyone at Camp Rock was talking about Tess's concert— as she was referring to it. Who else would perform? they wondered. Where would it take place? Which stars would come? How many people would read about it in a magazine or see it on TV?

It was all anyone could talk about, including Mitchie and Caitlyn. They sat alone at a table in the corner of the mess hall. Lola had skipped off for a drumming lesson, something she'd just taken up, and Peggy, perhaps curious to hear more about the concert, was sitting with Tess.

Since stepping out from behind Tess's shadow at Final Jam, Peggy floated around more. She hung out with Mitchie, Caitlyn, and Lola now, but she also spent time with her old friends Tess and Ella, and their new friend, Lorraine. She also still lived with Tess and the girls in the Vibe Cabin. At first, things had been awkward, but now it wasn't too bad.

Mitchie and Caitlyn didn't mind Peggy's dining choice. This gave them time to catch up. Besides the obvious news, Mitchie had a lot she wanted to share with Caitlyn. She had been at Camp Rock almost two whole sessions now and *still* hadn't won a jam. She was beginning to feel pretty bummed.

"Mitchie, you're talented," Caitlyn reassured

her once Mitchie had spilled what was on her mind. "Trust me. You have more talent in your pinkie finger than I have in my whole body," Caitlyn added.

"That's not true," Mitchie disagreed, frowning. "You're the best producer I know. You can do things with music on your computer that even the pros can't do!"

Caitlyn shrugged. She couldn't argue with that. She'd gotten even better this summer. Her laptop went with her everywhere, so when inspiration hit, she could begin work on songs in progress immediately.

Mitchie took a bite of her burger before continuing thoughtfully. "Sometimes I just wonder what it would be like to have all the advantages of someone born into the business."

"You mean like Tess?" Caitlyn asked, glancing over at Tess, who tossed her blond hair behind her shoulder as she answered more campers' questions about the concert.

She looked perfectly comfortable with all the attention.

"Well, not *exactly* like Tess," Mitchie said. "Just . . . haven't you ever wondered what life would be like if you were born someone else? In a different situation?"

"Of course," said Caitlyn. "Everyone does."

"That's all," Mitchie said with a sigh. "I just *wonder* what it would be like to be rock royalty."

Caitlyn thought about it for a second. "Weird," she decided.

Their conversation was interrupted when Mac walked up to the table.

"Hey, y'all mind if I sit down?" he asked in his soft North Carolina accent.

"Go ahead," Mitchie said brightly. She smiled mischievously at Caitlyn, who blushed and narrowed her eyes at her friend.

Mac sat down on the bench next to Caitlyn and smiled at her. "So, what do y'all think about Tess and this concert?" he asked. He waited, apparently very interested to hear Caitlyn's answer.

Caitlyn shrugged. "Tess seems pretty excited," she replied. She glanced again at Tess, who was now leaving the mess hall, trailed by Ella and Lorraine.

"I reckon I would be, too," replied Mac. "What do you think, Mitchie?"

"I think the cause is pretty cool," Mitchie observed. "To give kids who can't afford private classes—or places like Camp Rock—the opportunity to take music and singing lessons. I wish my school had a music program like that. We learned to play recorders in fourth grade, but that was about it."

"Me, too!" exclaimed Caitlyn. "I learned to play 'Hot Cross Buns.'"

"And 'Twinkle, Twinkle Little Star,'" remembered Mac, nodding.

All three of them laughed.

"So, um, you were into music even when

you were younger?" Mac asked Caitlyn, when the laughter had faded.

"Definitely," she answered. Looking up, she found Mac staring intently at her. He blushed and turned to Mitchie.

"What about you, Mitchie?" Mac asked, attempting to cover his embarrassment.

"I've been writing songs for as long as I can remember," she answered. "But it wasn't until this summer that I got up the guts to actually sing them for anyone."

Mac looked surprised. "Really? But you were great at B's Jam!"

For camp-director Brown's birthday every summer, Camp Rock had a special acoustic jam. This year, Mitchie hadn't won, but she'd definitely rocked the moment with one of her original songs.

"Thanks," Mitchie said with a shrug.

"And when you sang with Shane the other night at the B-Note," Mac added. "What's up with you two, by the way?"

Mitchie turned as red as the checkered tablecloth on the mess-hall table. "We're just friends," said Mitchie.

Mac sure is asking a lot of questions, Mitchie thought. He must just need an excuse to see Caitlyn. Too bad I have to be caught in the crossfire.

"*Good* friends," Caitlyn teased, poking Mitchie in the ribs.

Now it was Mitchie's turn to cut her eyes at Caitlyn, whose mouth had turned up into a playful smile.

"Shane and I are good friends," repeated Mitchie, hoping to put the subject to rest.

Mac nodded his head and looked as if he was about to ask her *another* question, but then reconsidered. Mitchie let out a sigh of relief. Mac was a really nice guy, but she could do without the third degree.

"And you?" Mac asked, once again turning his attention to Caitlyn. "Do you have any . . . good friends at home?" he asked carefully.

"Sure," Caitlyn said slyly. "I have lots of good friends."

"Oh," said Mac, his blond bangs falling into his blue eyes as he looked down at his hands.

"Sarah and Lindsay and Molly and Beth," explained Caitlyn. "They're not into music like I am, though."

Mac brightened, and Mitchie stifled a smile. She knew exactly why he had perked up. "Gotcha," he said cheerfully. "Well, are y'all heading down to B-Note now?"

"I am," Caitlyn said.

"Nope," answered Mitchie. "I'm finishing a new song. Think I'm going to head back to the cabin now." She stood to take her tray to the kitchen.

"Well," said Mac, turning to Caitlyn, "may I escort you to B-Note then?"

Like a gentleman from an old black-and-white movie, Mac held out his arm for Caitlyn to take. Caitlyn playfully slapped at it.

"I think I can escort myself," she said,

laughing. "But you can walk down there with me."

Mac gave Caitlyn an elated grin, and they both waved good-bye to Mitchie as she headed through the kitchen's double doors. She had to congratulate her mother on another terrific Camp Rock dinner.

CHAPTER THREE

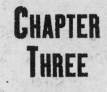

The next afternoon, Mitchie waited for Shane at their usual spot—the bench near the hollowed-out tree. He had asked if she would meet him there after dance class.

Mitchie had quickly agreed. She hadn't seen much of Shane lately. He and his bandmates, Nate and Jason, had been busy working with Andy Hosten and Colby on a song for Connect Three's new CD. As winners of the recent Musical Mystery Hunt, Colby and Andy had won more than just bragging rights—they'd be performing on a hidden track on Connect Three's next album.

Normally, Shane liked to write songs alone, or with Nate and Jason. But the collaboration with Colby and Andy was going better than he'd imagined. Now he was superexcited to share some of it with Mitchie.

Knowing that, Mitchie had to wonder why she'd been standing at the hollowed-out tree for almost ten minutes. Where was Shane? she thought as she checked her watch again. It wasn't like him to just not show. He hadn't pulled this kind of spoiled rock-star behavior since he first arrived at Camp Rock, when he was only there because his publicist thought it would be good for his image, not because he really wanted to be.

That wasn't the Shane Mitchie knew now. She was starting to worry that maybe he had been abducted by crazed fans when, suddenly, an acorn fell from the oak tree and landed next to her foot. Close call, she thought, as another acorn whizzed by her head. And another and another!

Mitchie glanced up into the branches of the tree. Did a squirrel have it in for her?

Apparently not. Through the leafy limbs, Mitchie spied something familiar—a pair of very stylish, dark sunglasses. Behind them was a grinning Shane. He had climbed the tree and was crouching on a thick branch, chuckling to himself as Mitchie jumped around dodging acorns.

"Hey!" Mitchie called up to Shane, pretending to be irritated. Secretly, though, she thought it was cute that Shane Gray, teen idol and pop sensation, was climbing trees like a little boy. "What's the big idea?"

Shane smoothly swung down from the branches and jumped to the ground next to Mitchie. He was still grinning.

"Did you think you were going *nuts* for a second?" he asked.

"Ba-dum-cha." Mitchie pretended to hit drums, teasing Shane about his lame joke.

He laughed. "Check it out. I'll be here all week, folks."

"So," Mitchie said, giving him a playful shove, "working with Colby and Andy is going well?"

Tucking her songwriting journal, which she had brought in case inspiration struck, under her arm, she and Shane began to walk toward the lake. They liked to take a canoe out on the water while they talked. It was peaceful out there. There was always so much *energy* around camp—with all the singing and dancing and music. Out on the water it was quiet, and Shane and Mitchie could be alone together.

"It's awesome," Shane answered enthusiastically. "They've got some great ideas—

different than mine, but really cool stuff."

"That's great," Mitchie said as she climbed into the shaky canoe. "I can't wait to hear it! Did you bring some of the lyrics?"

"All in here," said Shane, pointing at his head. He got in smoothly and pushed away from the shore with a paddle. They headed out toward the middle of the lake.

"Actually," he continued, "there's something else I wanted to tell you. You're the first person to know."

Mitchie raised an eyebrow. "The very first person?" she repeated with surprise. "Even before your agent?"

"Well, okay," he admitted. "He knows."

"And your publicist?"

Shane rolled his eyes. "Okay, she knows, too. But you're the first person to know at Camp Rock!"

"Well, that's something. What is it?" Mitchie asked eagerly. She liked that Shane felt he could confide in her.

"You know about the fund-raiser concert Tess and T. J. are in?"

"Yeah," said Mitchie. "Who doesn't?"

"Well, the organizers have asked me to perform, too."

"That's awesome, Shane!" Mitchie smiled wide. "Why?"

Shane faked a frown. "My sparkling personality and stand-up talent aren't reason enough?" he joked.

Mitchie splashed water at him. "No, goofball, I just meant how are you connected to School Rocks?"

"Before I got . . ." He paused.

"Famous," Mitchie continued for him.

Shane shook his head and continued. "Before I got *discovered*, I used to participate in a music program at my school. My old teacher is involved in the fund-raiser. He thought of me. They are recording the entire event, and all the proceeds from the CD sales go straight to the foundation. I think they're

23

even going to be selling shirts and programs and stuff."

Mitchie looked at Shane closely. How different he was in real life than she'd always imagined before she met him! The magazines and blogs always made him seem like a spoiled bad boy. But he was just like everyone else at Camp Rock—someone who had always just loved music, pure and simple.

"I think it's really cool that you're giving back," Mitchie said, seriously this time.

"One of the best parts of the job," replied Shane. He shrugged, a slight blush creeping over his face.

They were both quiet for a second. They could hear frogs croaking in the tall grass on the shore of the lake and someone singing in a cabin.

Then Shane brightened suddenly, as if he had an idea. "What about you?" he asked.

Mitchie looked confused. "What about me?"

"Well, you got to come to Camp Rock by helping your mom in the kitchen, right?"

Mitchie nodded. That was the deal. She couldn't have afforded it otherwise.

"Wouldn't you like to give someone else that chance, like your mom gave you?" asked Shane.

"Of course," said Mitchie.

"If you sing in the concert, maybe you could raise money for a Camp Rock scholarship. One lucky kid who participates in the School Rocks music program could come to Camp Rock each summer."

"*Me?* Sing in the concert?" Mitchie's eyes widened and she looked around and behind her. "I know you couldn't be talking about me, Shane Gray, because I could never sing in front of all those people. We're talking a major concert, Shane. In front of real live people with no connection to Camp Rock. Real live people who might be very happy to laugh at some no-name."

"But you wouldn't be alone," replied Shane. "You could sing with me. And according to you, I'm famous."

Mitchie considered this for a second. Stage fright aside, it would be *so* cool to give another camper the chance to come to Camp Rock. And it would be awesome to sing with Shane again.

"But . . ." she started to protest weakly.

"No ifs, ands, or buts," said Shane, as if he'd made up his mind. "I'll run it by Uncle Brown tonight. See if he approves the scholarship idea."

"All right," said Mitchie, nodding her head.

She beamed as Shane picked up the oars and steered them back to shore. The sun was setting behind him and the water glowed.

"Talk about a good canoe ride!" Shane said a moment later. "You're performing at the concert with me in Los Angeles, and we're starting a Camp Rock scholarship!"

Mitchie's smile vanished instantly. "Los Angeles?" she asked.

"Yeah," said Shane as he rowed. In the growing shadows, he couldn't see that the smile had faded from Mitchie's face. "The concert is being held at Grauman's Chinese Theater—a national landmark!"

"I can't go to L.A., Shane," said Mitchie. "My mom would never let me."

"Not even with a chaperone?" Shane asked hopefully.

Mitchie shook her head. "Probably not."

"Well, it doesn't hurt to ask," Shane said, keeping the hope alive.

"You're right," said Mitchie doubtfully. "It doesn't hurt to ask. I'll check first thing tomorrow, before breakfast."

"I'm sure she'll say yes," Shane said. "Connie's always liked me."

"Connie?" Mitchie asked, eyeing him. "You're on a first-name basis with my mother now?"

"Mrs. Torres." Shane grinned. "If that will get her to let you come to Los Angeles."

Mitchie laughed. These moments with Shane were some of Mitchie's favorite times at camp.

But she and Shane weren't alone. At the far end of the long line of canoes pulled up onshore, someone lay in the bottom of one of them, listening as Shane and Mitchie excitedly discussed which song they would perform at the concert.

"What about that song you wrote a couple weeks ago?" Shane asked.

"No. It's not ready yet," said Mitchie. "But what about your song, 'Hectic'?"

Hidden in the bottom of the canoe, the eavesdropper scribbled the word "Hectic" on a pad of paper.

"No," said Shane. "I think the tempo's too fast for this event. But you know what I think would be perfect?"

"What?" asked Mitchie, straining as she

28

and Shane beached their canoe.

"The song you sang at B's Jam," answered Shane.

The person in the boat scratched out "Hectic" and wrote "This Place."

"I couldn't," Mitchie said. "Not in front of all those people!"

"You could," said Shane, putting his arm around Mitchie. "Remember, I'll be right there with you!"

The person in the boat, still unnoticed by Shane and Mitchie as they left the lake for their respective cabins, scribbled furiously.

Once he was sure Mitchie and Shane were out of sight, the observer sat up. It was Mac! "My editors are gonna *love* this," he said, smiling. Slowly, he got up and headed back to his cabin, his cover safe for now.

What no one knew at Camp Rock was that Mac wasn't there as a budding rock star; he was there as a budding rock journalist. And he had just uncovered a *major* scoop!

CHAPTER FOUR

When Mitchie had bounded in to her cabin and told Caitlyn about the fund-raising concert, Caitlyn had thought it was a great idea. So had Brown when Shane asked him about it.

The next morning, however, Connie Torres was not as convinced.

"I'm sorry, honey. It's just too far. I can't go with you to L.A. because I have to stay here and feed the camp," Connie said as she stirred a giant bowl of waffle batter. "Plus, it's probably very expensive."

"What about Dad?" pleaded Mitchie.

Her mother thought for a second, as if that might work, but then her face fell and she shook her head. "He's in Florida for business that week," she said, remembering.

Connie looked genuinely disappointed for her daughter, but it just wasn't going to work out. She couldn't let Mitchie run off by herself with a rock star to Los Angeles for the weekend!

Mitchie picked glumly at the bowl of blueberries in front of her, but she'd lost her appetite.

"I'm sorry, honey," her mother said again when Mitchie remained silent.

Mitchie nodded—she knew her mother was sorry, but that didn't make it stink any less. Mitchie rose slowly from the table. It was time for breakfast, and the rest of the campers were beginning to file into the mess hall. Pushing through the doors, Mitchie walked from the kitchen into the dining room to join her friends.

"So, what'd she say?" Peggy asked as Mitchie plopped down at a table with Caitlyn, Peggy, Colby, and Mac.

Mitchie looked over at Peggy with a large frown. "Does my face answer your question?" she asked.

"I guess that's a no . . ." Caitlyn said, sighing. "Too bad, Mitchie. I'm sorry. That's a bummer. It would have been a pretty unbelievable experience."

"Yeah," said Mitchie. "It would have been. I guess I should look on the bright side, though."

"What's that?" Colby asked.

Mitchie wrinkled her forehead. "I'm not sure!" She laughed. "But I'll try and find one . . . eventually."

Mitchie attempted to eat some eggs, but by the time Brown thumped on a microphone at the end of breakfast to get everyone's attention, they were still a yellow, rubbery mound on her plate. The news had taken away her appetite.

Thump, thump, thump. Slowly, glasses and silverware stopped clinking, and the campers grew quiet as they waited for the director to speak.

"Thank you," Brown said. "And good morning! I have a special announcement to make."

Now the dining hall was *really* quiet. When Brown said "special" announcement, he usually meant super special.

"I'm excited to tell you that I got a call from T.J. Tyler last night." At the mention of her mother, Tess beamed. "The theater in L.A. that was going to host the School Rocks concert unfortunately had to back out."

A whisper rippled through the room as campers turned to look at Tess, expecting her face to fall as she realized the concert was off. The smile stayed, frozen on her lips.

Brown continued. "But the concert is still on. It's just moving a little." He paused. "To our very own backyard. The concert will now be held in town—at Lincoln High School. And we are *all* invited to attend!"

Applause burst from the crowd. Ecstatic and wide-eyed, Mitchie looked at all her friends.

"This means you *can* perform in the concert!" Mac exclaimed.

"I guess so," said Mitchie. "I can't believe it!"

"Well, believe it, girl," Peggy said. "'Cause this isn't a dream."

Before she could say more, Brown tapped on the microphone again. Apparently there *was* more news.

"Since this was such short notice for Lincoln High, I've volunteered you all to help." Groans rang out. "Tone it down," he said. "It just means you'll be helping with

34

the set and decorations. And just in case we get any foot traffic, Dee has been put in charge of sprucing up the place."

His announcement done, Brown walked off, leaving a noisy—and excited—roomful of campers behind.

With only one day until the concert, all of Camp Rock was mobilized to prepare. Dee La Duke, the camp music director, organized a campwide trash pickup. Every cabin had to bring her as many candy wrappers, soda cans, and pieces of litter as they could find. Discarded guitar picks counted double. The cabin that collected the most trash would win an ice-cream party in B-Note.

A select group of campers was placed on decoration duty and headed into town. They followed the directions of the School Rocks event design coordinator to transform Lincoln High's theater into an A-list concert-worthy auditorium. Red carpets were laid down along the aisles. Streamers were strung from the rafters, and Barron James and Sander Loya were in charge of rigging a balloon-and-confetti drop from the ceiling.

Amidst it all, Tess reigned, acting as the pop princess she knew she was destined to be. "Barron!" Tess shouted from the stage. Barron and Sander were balancing on the scaffolding above her. "Are those red balloons?"

"Sure are," Sander affirmed.

"But my outfit's pink," Tess said.

"And your point . . . ?" Barron asked.

"Red clashes with pink," Tess said with an exaggerated sigh.

"You can wear the turquoise, strappy dress from my costume trunk instead," offered Lorraine, who was, as always, standing close by Tess.

"Isn't that the dress you were going to wear, Lorraine?" Peggy asked.

"Well, yeah," Lorraine said, shrugging.

"But I'm happy to let Tess wear it if she wants."

Mac had also pulled decorating duty and was standing nearby. "No need!" he said. "Red and pink is actually the color combo of the moment, according to *Celeb Beat* magazine."

"Really?" Ella asked.

Mac nodded.

"Oh, yeah," Tess said thoughtfully. "I think I remember reading that, now that you mention it. Red balloons are fine, Sander. Proceed!" Tess shouted up to the guys rigging the balloons.

"What?" Barron yelled back down. As he did, a cascade of red balloons tumbled from the rafters and landed on top of Tess.

Ella, Lorraine, and Mac laughed, but Tess scowled.

"Oh, come on, Tess," Mac said gently. "You have to admit, that was kinda funny."

Not immune to Mac's Southern charm,

Tess's lips cracked into a smile and she finally started laughing. Their giggles were interrupted by Caitlyn and a School Rocks stagehand approaching Mac.

"Hey," said Caitlyn. "Bob here needs help leading the wires from the sound booth to the stage. You think you could help?"

"Sure!" Mac cried.

"And we need one more person," said Caitlyn, looking at the others who were standing around.

"Ella's really good at that stuff, too," Mac said.

Ella blushed at the compliment. "Sure, I can help," she offered.

"Great," replied Caitlyn. "Let's follow Bob."

The three followed the stagehand, who was dressed all in black even though the show wasn't for another day, down the stage stairs and to the back of the theater.

As Caitlyn helped Bob with a jumble of wires and checked the sound using the various buttons and levers on the sound-board, Mac looked on in wonder.

"You really know your stuff," Mac said as Caitlyn fiddled with the equipment.

"It's not all that different from my computer," Caitlyn said.

"I'm not so good with computers," Mac replied.

"How can you not be good with computers?" Caitlyn asked, sounding genuinely confused. "You *are* aware that you live in the twenty-first century, right?"

"Well, I figured they were just a passing fad." Mac flashed a joking smile.

Caitlyn laughed. "Are you on Facebook? Or MySpace? IM?"

"I might consider it if you are," Mac said.

Caitlyn turned a deep shade of red. She had no idea what to say. And normally she was the first with a witty comeback! "Okay, Bob," she said instead, speaking into a microphone to distract herself, "I think we're all set here.

Mac and I will start running wires down to the stage."

On the stage, there was a flurry of excitement. Mitchie and Shane had just arrived for their sound check, and both the School Rocks PR team and stage crew were bustling around them.

"Which angle do you think is her best?" someone shouted to a camera operator.

"Red filters on the lights will look fabulous with Mitchie's hair," a stylist observed from the sidelines.

The PR team had gone all out for the event, hiring everyone who was anyone in the business. When the event got press—and it would—School Rocks wanted its stars looking terrific.

"Oooh," gushed a makeup person. "And I can put some pink highlighting around her cheekbones to make her eyes pop."

Listening to everyone talk about her as if she weren't there, Mitchie stood, frozen to the spot. "I'm not sure I want my eyes to pop," she whispered to Shane. "That sounds like it hurts."

Shane chuckled, but Mitchie was serious. She wasn't sure how to handle all this attention. So she just stood still as people fluttered around her, touching her hair and her clothes, positioning her on the stage, and setting her microphone to the right height.

Repeatedly, she shot Shane a look that cried, "Help me!"

"Do you like the mike here?" an assistant asked Mitchie. He lowered the microphone two inches. "Or here?"

Mitchie thought about it. "Um . . . here, I guess."

"Shane," someone else asked, "do you think you should be more upstage?"

Shane looked at Mitchie. "What do you think?"

Mitchie shrugged. "More downstage."

The more questions the "talent handlers" asked, the more comfortable Mitchie became with giving orders. By the time the actual sound check commenced, Mitchie was enjoying herself. It was a whirlwind, but she had to admit . . . it was kind of fun to be at the center of it all.

CHAPTER FIVE

Two electric mixers, a blender, and three burners on the stove in the kitchen were going when Mitchie got back to camp. Once again, her mom was swamped. With the concert, she not only had to feed the camp but Brown had also volunteered her services to the School Rocks' staff.

Luckily, Caitlyn had stopped by looking for Mitchie and when she saw the chaos, offered to lend Connie a hand. Now she was chopping cucumbers at the large kitchen table as she told Connie about the changes to the school's theater.

They both looked up as the door slammed behind Mitchie. She looked at her mom and friend and shrugged sheepishly. She knew she was late, but the sound check had gone on forever.

"Sorry! Sorry!" Mitchie cried, warding off a scolding from her mother about being on time by giving her a kiss on the cheek and quickly taking a seat next to Caitlyn. Picking up a cucumber, she began to chop.

"So, how'd it go?" her mom asked. She had been thrilled when Brown made his announcement—despite the extra work it meant. Seeing her daughter happy was well worth it.

"It went really well," Mitchie answered.

Connie smiled broadly. She knew how Mitchie could get nervous performing in front of a lot of people. But Mitchie had been working on getting past that all summer, and it seemed to be paying off.

"That's great, sweetie," Connie said, wiping her hands on her apron, which was already splattered with food.

"It was great—and all about *you*," Caitlyn teased. She and Mac had watched the crew flutter around Mitchie and Shane from the sound booth. "You should have seen the look on Tess's face!"

Mitchie shrugged. "Really? I mean I guess the crew was kind of attentive." She finished chopping one cucumber and picked up another.

"You *guess*? They were all," Caitlyn imitated the staff, "'lights on her hair' and 'let's make her eyes pop.'"

Mitchie laughed and rolled her eyes. "I know. They just want it to be perfect, though. You can't blame them. . . . I mean, I want it to be perfect, too. This is the official kick-off of the Camp Rock scholarship!"

Mitchie's mom weighed in from the sink. "I think it's wonderful that you've found a way to give back to Camp Rock, Mitchie."

"Well, it was Shane's idea, really," Mitchie reminded her.

"I knew I liked that boy," Mitchie's mom joked, her brown eyes twinkling.

"Anyway," Mitchie continued, changing the subject, "I can only stay for a little bit today, Mom. We have a wardrobe fitting at—" Mitchie glanced at her watch. "Shoot! In ten minutes."

Mitchie swiped the cucumbers she had diced into a neat pile beside Caitlyn's.

"You have to go?" Caitlyn and Connie asked at the same time.

"Whoa—jinx! You owe each other a Coke." Mitchie was laughing, but her mother wasn't.

"Mitchie, I'm going crazy in here with all this extra food I have to make," Connie said, running a hand through her brown hair. "I need you in the kitchen."

"But they have to fit me for my wardrobe," Mitchie explained again.

"Well, can't you reschedule for later in the day?" her mom asked. "Like *after* lunch?"

"There's a makeup meeting after the fitting," Mitchie said, unaware that her tone had become a little condescending.

Caitlyn's gaze bounced between mother and daughter, all too aware of the growing tension.

Connie eyed her daughter. What had gotten into Mitchie? The most makeup she wore at home was Chap Stick!

"And then I'm scheduled for a mani," Mitchie added, almost as an afterthought.

"'A mani'?" Connie repeated, not sure she was hearing correctly.

Even Caitlyn was beginning to feel confused by this imposter Mitchie.

47

"Too 'mani' excuses," Caitlyn muttered under her breath, but either Mitchie didn't hear her or didn't care.

"A manicure," Mitchie explained. "I can't go onstage as a School Rocks representative with dishpan hands!" She held up her hands for proof. It was true. Her nail polish was chipped, and her hands looked dried out from the dish soap they used every day in the kitchen.

Connie sighed. "Okay. I just hope your other beauty appointments don't interfere with dinner prep."

As Connie spoke, the sound of a cell phone ringing filled the kitchen. It was coming from Mitchie's pocket.

"Oh! Just a second," said Mitchie, extracting her phone from her pocket. "Hello?" she chirped.

As Mitchie talked to whoever was on the other line, Caitlyn and Connie exchanged glances.

"Since when has Mitchie carried her cell

phone at camp?" Connie asked Caitlyn.

"Apparently since she became rock royalty," Caitlyn said with a groan. Funny how quickly things can change, she thought.

"That was Ginger," Mitchie said, as if that were obvious. Neither Caitlyn nor Connie knew Ginger, the creative director of the School Rocks concert. "They're waiting for me at the Keynote Cabin. Sorry to jet!" Waving good-bye, Mitchie flew out the door.

"I'll stay and help you, Connie," said Caitlyn.

"Thank you, Caitlyn."

"Connie?" Caitlyn said hesitantly a few minutes later.

"Hmmm?" Connie responded as she diced tomatoes.

"Do you think Mitchie remembers that the only reason she's at Camp Rock is because *you* offered to work in the kitchen?"

Connie sighed. "That's a good question, Caitlyn. That's a very good question."

As they chopped and diced and slivered and sautéed, they both wondered how Mitchie, of all people, could have morphed into a demi-diva overnight.

There was one big challenge at a place like Camp Rock, where you were performing all the time—to keep your music fresh. So Caitlyn, after kitchen duty, had wandered over to an empty rehearsal cabin to work on some new material.

She was trying to get the hook of a new song down, but whatever she was doing wasn't working. Caitlyn was so engrossed in her computer that she didn't even hear the sound of footsteps approaching.

"Oh, my gosh, you scared me!" Caitlyn nearly jumped out of her skin when she noticed Mac standing behind her.

"Not exactly the reaction I was going for." Mac grinned. "May I?" He gestured to the bench next to Caitlyn.

Caitlyn stifled a laugh. Mac could be so formal sometimes. "You may," she said dramatically.

"What are you workin' on today?" Mac drawled.

"I'm trying to get this hook down, but something's off."

"Can I have a listen?" he asked.

"Sure."

Mac reached across and punched ENTER on Caitlyn's laptop. Designs on the screen danced in neon shades of pink, green, and blue as the music played. It was good, but she was right, the hook was off.

"Yeah. That doesn't work," agreed Mac.

"Gee, thanks," Caitlyn said sarcastically. She slumped on the bench and ran a hand through her wavy brown hair.

"I tried this." Caitlyn punched some keys and the hook played again. Still not right. "And this." Again, no good.

Caitlyn fidgeted with a leather bracelet on

her wrist and sighed. "I just can't seem to concentrate," she grumbled.

"Why not? Are you distracted?"

"What would I be distracted by?" Caitlyn responded.

"Something . . . or someone?" Caitlyn didn't pick up on the hint of hopefulness in Mac's voice. Although he wouldn't dare admit it out loud, he was hoping *he* might be the one occupying Caitlyn's thoughts.

"Yes!" Caitlyn exclaimed. It was as if a lightbulb had suddenly turned on in her head. "That's exactly it."

"Really?" Mac asked, surprised and pleased. But then Caitlyn went on.

"It's Mitchie," she said. "She's not acting like herself, and it's kind of throwing me for a loop."

"Oh," Mac said, hiding his disappointment. "I see. . . . So, what's she acting like?"

"A diva," Caitlyn explained. "All day, with this concert, she's been acting like a total pop princess. That's *so* not Mitchie."

"I hear ya," Mac said. "She must be under a lot of pressure, though. A lot has happened this summer, and now she's performing at a huge promotional concert with Shane Gray! That would make anyone act a little differently."

Caitlyn considered Mac's words for a moment. "You're right," she said finally. "Hopefully once the concert's over, her head will shrink back down to normal size."

Mac laughed.

"You know," observed Caitlyn, "you're pretty easy to talk to."

Mac's cheeks flushed. "Thanks," he said, looking at Caitlyn's screen saver as if it were the most interesting thing in the world. "You're pretty easy to talk to yourself."

"Thanks." Caitlyn sighed. "Too bad my superior conversational skills won't fix my hook." She turned back to her laptop.

"What if . . ." Mac said, then his voice trailed off. "Never mind."

"What?" Caitlyn asked. She wanted his opinion.

"What if you use a B-flat here and speed up the tempo there?" Mac pointed to the chord progression on the laptop's screen.

Caitlyn hummed the tune. "Yes!" she cried. "I like that. That works."

She punched a few keys on her computer, and the music played again. The beat was stronger, and the hook actually hooked the listener.

"Thanks." Caitlyn grinned at Mac, and he grinned back.

"No problem," he said.

Caitlyn didn't know what to say now. Her heart was racing oddly and her palms felt unnaturally clammy. Mac looked nervous, too.

Suddenly, they were interrupted by a sound outside the rehearsal cabin. It sounded like someone was crying—a girl. Standing up, Caitlyn went to the cabin's window and peered outside. Tess was sitting on the front steps.

Why is it that *I* always seem to be the one finding Tess in tears? Caitlyn mused to herself. But she quickly pushed that thought aside. Tess looked really upset.

"Tess?" Caitlyn said softly, trying not to startle her. Turning, Tess looked like a deer caught in headlights. She quickly wiped the tears from her cheeks. "Oh. Hey, Caitlyn." She stood up. "I was just leaving."

"Hang on," said Caitlyn, running across the cabin and out the door onto the front porch with Tess. "What's up? Is something wrong?"

Tess bit her bottom lip and shook her blond head. "No," she said. "Why would you think that?"

Mac had come outside and joined them on the front porch.

"Umm . . . maybe because you're crying?" Caitlyn said, trying not to sound too sarcastic. She knew Tess's guard went up quickly.

Tess sucked in her lower lip and looked up at the blue sky. It was obvious she was trying to stop crying, but a tear slid down her cheek anyway. "Fine," she said, deciding she couldn't hide it this time. "I'm just upset because I found out something about the concert."

"What'd you find out?" Mac asked, leaning against a wood post.

Tess took a deep breath. She barely knew Mac and didn't exactly get along with Caitlyn, but she had to tell someone. If she didn't, she was afraid she'd be teary—and blotchy—forever. "One of the concert organizers slipped and said that they only invited me to perform because my mom *made* them," she spat.

Tess tried to look really mad but couldn't. Instead, her bottom lip trembled and her eyes filled with more tears.

Caitlyn looked at Mac, unsure of what to do. He shrugged, as if to say, "I have no clue, it's a girl thing." Moving closer to Tess, Caitlyn awkwardly put an arm around the girl's shoulders.

"It's okay, Tess," Caitlyn said, trying to sound reassuring. "It doesn't matter how you got on the lineup. You're totally gonna rock the concert. That's all that matters!"

Tess sniffled.

Caitlyn was saved from having to offer more advice by Ella.

"Tess?" the other girl said, coming up the path toward the rehearsal cabin. Lorraine was right beside her.

Hearing Ella's voice, Tess pulled out from under Caitlyn's arm and quickly wiped her eyes.

"Oh, hey, Ella," Tess said casually, spinning to face them. Her "plastic" face was on again. "What's up?"

"Were you crying?" Lorraine asked, looking concerned and confused.

"No," Tess said quickly. "A bug just flew in

my eye. Caitlyn and Mac were helping me get it out."

Tess shot the pair a look, daring them to contradict her.

"Yeah," Mac said. "We were just helping her get a gnat out of her lie—I mean *eye*."

Caitlyn giggled but said nothing.

Tess gave them one last look and then walked off the porch. "Thanks, Caitlyn," she said over her shoulder as she headed toward the path that led to the lake, Ella and Lorraine on either side. Her moment of vulnerability was apparently over.

Caitlyn sighed as Tess disappeared around the bend. When she looked at Mac, they both doubled over in laughter.

"'Out of her *lie*?'" repeated Caitlyn.

Mac grinned. "Couldn't help it."

"It's all fun and games until someone loses a lie, you know," Caitlyn cracked.

"I guess you and I see lie to lie on the matter," Mac joked.

"I'm keeping my lie on you, Wilson," Caitlyn teased.

"Fine by me!" said Mac. "I've been keeping mine on you."

Caitlyn blushed. She never thought she'd say this, but it seemed Mac's Southern charm was working. For a little while, she'd forgotten that her best friend had done a personality switch. Caitlyn just hoped that diva Mitchie would disappear as quickly as she had appeared.

CHAPTER SIX

The next morning, Mitchie's eyes shot open before her alarm clock even rang to wake her for kitchen duty. She had barely slept at all. It was the day of the School Rocks concert. Today she, Mitchie Torres, would sing on a stage in front of total strangers. Gulp. How am I going to do this? she wondered.

Luckily, there was quite a lot going on to keep her mind preoccupied. Mitchie spent most of the day in town at the school for a final sound check and rehearsal under the enthusiastic watch of Brown and Dee. Then it was off to wardrobe and hair and makeup before she had to be backstage at three. They were "rolling," as the crew said, at six.

In addition to the crew and School Rocks organizers, the high-school grounds were also swarming with T.J. Tyler's entourage, including the president of Blush Cosmetics, who followed T.J. around like a puppy, telling her how "fabulous" she was at least every two minutes.

Nate and Jason had come to support Shane. Over the summer they had made several trips to Camp Rock and Mitchie was glad to see them there. She needed all the familiar faces she could get in the audience.

By five, the high school's theater was packed with campers, counselors, Lincoln students and friends, a few select members of the press, and special guests of the performers and School Rocks. Outside the theater, cashiers rang up last-minute sales of T-shirts, mugs, programs, and other concert paraphernalia. The show's producers were making final adjustments, while stagehands bustled back and forth talking to each other about set changes, lighting, and microphone placement over their headsets.

Meanwhile, in the wings, Mitchie paced. It felt like a cage full of butterflies had been unleashed in her stomach. Shane was waiting with her and was far less nervous. To him, this was just another day "on the job." But he knew Mitchie was upset, and he was trying to calm her.

"Deep breaths," he said. "Hee-hee-hoo. Hee-hee-hoo," he breathed in and out.

"You sound silly!" Mitchie laughed.

"See, but you're smiling now. That's better than hyperventilating."

"True," Mitchie said, peeking around the red curtain. In the third row sat Lola, Peggy, and Colby, and on the end was Caitlyn, next to Mac. Behind them, she could make out Barron, Sander, and Andy. She heaved a deep sigh.

"You're gonna be great," said Shane, putting his hands on Mitchie's shoulders and turning her to face him. He looked deep in her eyes. "If you get nervous, just remember to look at me."

"I might end up looking at you the whole time," said Mitchie.

"That's fine with me," Shane said, smiling. "Ready for your big moment?"

Mitchie spun around at the familiar, deep voice. "Dad!" she cried. Rushing over, she flew into her father's waiting arms. Beside him, Connie smiled.

"Whoa," he said, nearly bowled over by her momentum.

Mitchie looked in surprise between her mother and father. "I thought you were working!"

"I was," he said. "But I couldn't miss seeing my daughter's big moment."

"How did you get backstage?" Mitchie asked. She glanced at the muscular bodyguards in tight black T-shirts guarding all the entrances to the stage. "The security here's like Fort Knox tonight!"

"We know people," her mom joked. "I told them Mitchie Torres was my daughter."

"Plus, Brown vouched for us," her dad added.

"I'm so happy to see you!" Mitchie cried. She hugged her mom and dad again.

Beside her, Shane quietly cleared his throat.

"Oh, sorry! Dad, you remember Shane Gray." Earlier that summer they had met briefly after Final Jam.

"Nice to see you again, Mr. Torres," Shane said politely. Mitchie was impressed. He even held out his hand to shake her father's.

"Likewise," said Mr. Torres. "I've heard you and Mitchie have been having a great summer."

Shane blanched. "From the tabloids?"

"No, from Mitchie's mom," Mitchie's dad answered. Shane laughed and relaxed.

"You know, in all the craziness, I never thought to ask—what song are you singing?" Mitchie's mom asked.

"'This Place,'" Mitchie and Shane answered in unison.

"It's the one I wrote for B's Jam," explained Mitchie. "The acoustic song about Camp Rock that Faye Hart wanted to buy but I didn't want to sell."

"I asked if we could sing it, since it's about camp," Shane added. "And part of the money we raise *is* going toward the Camp Rock scholarship." He turned to Mr. Torres. "I don't know if Mrs. Torres told you, but Mitchie's really been an inspiration."

"So I heard," said Mitchie's dad, nodding his head appreciatively.

Suddenly, a stagehand hurried up, all business. "Five minutes till you're on," she warned. She looked at Mitchie's parents. "Are you her manager?" she asked Connie.

"No. I'm her mother," Connie replied.

"Okay, well if you're not staff, you're going to have to leave the stage," she said, shuffling the Torreses toward the stairs. "Sorry."

"Good luck, honey!" Mitchie's dad called over his shoulder.

"No!" Connie said, playfully hitting him on the arm. "You're supposed to say 'break a leg.'"

"Oh, right. Go and break a leg, honey!" he called, correcting himself.

Mitchie watched them go, wishing she could see them in the audience when she was onstage. But she knew that once all the lights were on, all she would see was a big empty space. Her face went pale.

"Are you okay?" Shane asked.

"Yeah," Mitchie said. "No. I think I might be sick." She leaned over, her hands on her knees, and took deep breaths.

"Excuse me," Shane said, stopping a crew member as he walked by. "Mitchie needs a paper bag."

"And maybe some water," Mitchie added, hunched over.

"Any special kind?" the crew member said.

"Of bag?" Mitchie asked.

The stagehand rolled his eyes. "Of water."

"Oh. Whatever." Mitchie just wanted something with two molecules of hydrogen and one molecule of oxygen. Anything to keep her from fainting.

Meanwhile, on the other side of the stage, Tess was having her own case of nerves. She'd never been this anxious before a performance. Of course, she'd never performed for such a big event before, either. But she'd watched her mother do it a thousand times, so it couldn't be that hard. You just looked at the audience and sang, right? So why did Tess also feel like she was going to throw up?

"Tess, you look a little pasty," T.J. said as

Tess watched a stagehand count down on his fingers.

"Five, four, three," he said, and then went silent for two and one. He pointed at the stage.

The audience in Lincoln High's theater erupted into applause as the chairwoman of School Rocks and the president of Blush Cosmetics took the stage to introduce the cause and the acts.

"Honey, are you feeling okay?" T.J. asked, putting her hand to Tess's forehead.

"I'm fine," said Tess, shrugging her off. "Just a little nervous, that's all."

"You mean stage fright?" her mom asked.

Tess nodded. "I guess so."

"It'll go away the minute you step onstage," T.J. assured her. "Trust me."

Tess wasn't sure. However, she didn't have much time to worry about it. A stage tech was urgently cueing T.J. and Tess to take their places onstage.

As Tess and her mom took their positions,

smoke machines whirred into action. A huge backdrop with the initials T & T on it descended from the rafters. The audience oohed and ahhed as brightly colored lights danced across the stage.

Here goes, thought Tess.

"To benefit School Rocks, please give a warm welcome to T. J. Tyler and her daughter, Tess!" someone announced, and the music started. It thrummed through the boards of the old stage floor. It was a beat Tess had heard a thousand times before—her mother's hit song, "Queen for a Day."

As the music engulfed her, Tess's nerves disappeared, and the words spilled out of her as she hit all her cues. She nailed the choreography and belted out the chorus, grinning from ear to ear. She couldn't see a thing with the lights, but she knew the audience— including kids who would benefit from any money raised—was out there watching her. And even better, she was singing with her mom. It was the best feeling in the world.

When the song ended, the lights went out and Tess stood, trying to catch her breath.

"Great job, Tess," her mom whispered. She was grateful for the opportunity to bond with her daughter. They saw so little of each other when she was on tour. "You ready for a few more?"

"Bring it," Tess said.

By the end of their set, Tess was sweating from the bright lights, but she had never been happier. She bounded off the stage.

"And *that*," she said to Shane and Mitchie, who were waiting their turn to go on after a few more words from their sponsors, "is how School Rocks."

"Awesome performance, Tess," said Mitchie. It had been pretty spectacular—the lights, the smoke, the glitter. It was a performance fit for rock royalty. Mitchie just hoped she wouldn't look like the court jester following the Tylers. . . .

As if reading Mitchie's mind, Tess flicked her hair and said, "I know." The diva was back—until Tess suddenly realized a recording device was set up close by. "Good luck!" she added, changing her tone. She threw her arms around Mitchie for an insincere hug.

Just then the announcer introduced Mitchie and Shane. Any butterflies Mitchie had felt performing at jams or concerts this summer were teeny compared to the giant ones she felt fluttering in her stomach now.

Shane could see Mitchie's anxiety growing. Right before they were cued to take their positions onstage, Shane took Mitchie's hand. She was pale and wide-eyed, and he turned her so she was facing him. "Ignore the audience, Mitchie. Ignore the recorders. Just look at me. Just sing like you mean it."

Mitchie nodded. Infused with Shane's confidence, they ran onstage together. He squeezed her hand as the bass started.

At first, Mitchie winced in the bright lights, but as she looked into Shane's eyes, she forgot about everything, and just concentrated on the words to her song. She thought about how much she loved Camp Rock, and how happy she would be if she could help someone else attend. And slowly, under the glare of the lights, it began to feel as if she and Shane were the only people on Earth.

As they finished, the audience exploded in applause. Their performance was pitch-perfect. Mitchie could have kept going, but T.J. and Tess were the main act, so it was time to take a bow and let them perform again.

As Shane and Mitchie exited the stage, Mitchie felt as though she was floating on air. She was so relieved and happy that she didn't even mind when a pack of reporters and photographers mobbed them backstage. They began hurling questions at them, especially at Mitchie.

"Did you write that song?"

"Yes."

"Did Shane help you?"

"No, but he inspired me . . ."

"Are you and Shane an item?

Mitchie blushed. What was she supposed to say? Luckily, Shane was used to these questions and jumped in. "No comment," he said. "Next question."

"Let's see you pose for a photo together!" a photographer shouted.

Shane and Mitchie mugged for the cameras, side by side. A prince and his princess. A short while later, Tess and T.J. came up, wanting their share of the spotlight. The four of them smiled as the cameras flashed. Of course, Tess made sure to get in front of Mitchie whenever she could.

Caitlyn, Lola, and Mac had managed to sneak backstage with a little help from the stagehand Caitlyn had worked with the day before. From the shadows on the side of the stage, they watched Mitchie hold court.

Caitlyn sighed. "I really hope once the concert's over we get our old Mitchie back again."

"We will," assured Lola.

"Can I quote you on that?" Mac asked.

Lola and Caitlyn laughed.

If they had known Mac was serious, they probably wouldn't have been giggling. But Mac *was* serious. In a few hours he was supposed to file a report on the fund-raiser with his editor at *Celeb Beat*. And from what he could tell, it was shaping up to be quite a story.

CHAPTER SEVEN

Mitchie fished a bulb of garlic from the kitchen's vegetable bin and set to work peeling the garlic's papery, white skin.

Outside the kitchen window, she could hear Barron and Sander practicing a new rap song they'd been working on. From the other window came the sound of someone practicing a drum solo. Normal, everyday sounds at Camp Rock.

"I need six cloves in total," her mother called over her shoulder to Mitchie.

"Hmm?" Mitchie asked. Her mind wasn't exactly on her work. It had been two days since the School Rocks fund-raiser, and Mitchie still couldn't think of anything else.

"Six cloves," her mom repeated. She looked sideways at her daughter. "Earth to Mitchie."

Mitchie laughed as she placed the six cloves on the counter to crush. "Sorry," she answered dreamily. "I'm just thinking about the concert."

Her mother smiled and continued stirring the chili on the stove. "It did go really well," Connie confirmed, marveling once again at her daughter's star performance.

"Really?" Mitchie pressed.

They'd been over this a dozen times since that night. Mitchie just couldn't believe that a) it had happened; b) it was over; and c) she really hadn't fallen flat on her face and/or forgotten every word to the song.

"Yes! It was great," her mom reassured her for the umpteenth time. "*You* were great."

"I was, wasn't I?" Mitchie joked, batting her eyelashes and grinning.

The room grew silent as Mitchie and Connie went back to their chopping. The dishwasher and refrigerator hummed, and, for a moment, all was peaceful.

"Shoot!" Mitchie suddenly exclaimed, breaking the silence.

"What?" her mother gasped, darting across the kitchen in a flash, thinking Mitchie had cut herself.

Mitchie was examining her hands. "My manicure is totally chipping from all this peeling and chopping." Mitchie frowned and raised her hands to her face. "And I reek of garlic. No one's going to want to stand downwind of me!"

Connie raised an eyebrow. She had been sure Mitchie would snap out of her new high-maintenance ways after the concert. But since then, Mitchie had been less interested in helping in the kitchen and more interested in the world's reaction to the concert—and in herself.

Connie knew Mitchie had been secretly using the computer in the office to check the gossip blogs and Web sites that covered the show. Most of the stories focused on T.J.'s presence at the event and the huge amount of money it had raised. But every few articles, there was a shout-out to Mitchie and her performance with Shane. Connie knew it was all understandable—the concert had been a huge deal for her daughter. But still, Mitchie's behavior lately was just not very . . . Mitchie. Her mom wondered if Mitchie remembered why she'd gotten involved in the concert in the first place—for the scholarship to help kids like herself who normally couldn't afford a summer at Camp Rock.

Unaware of her mom's musings, Mitchie

ran her hands under the faucet, scrubbing with soap at the last pieces of garlic. She dried them on her apron and slid the straps over her head.

"Where are you going?" her mother asked. She still had to prepare the fresh veggies for the salad bar, and Mitchie usually helped with that.

Mitchie's eyes widened innocently. "Shane wants to show me the YouTube video of the concert," she said. "You don't mind, do you?"

Connie put her hand on her hip and looked at her daughter. "Mitchie Torres," she said suspiciously, "what's gotten into you? You remember the deal: you get to come to Camp Rock, but I need your help in the kitchen."

"Mommm," Mitchie whined. "I *am* helping. But isn't the whole point of me coming to Camp Rock to jump-start my career?"

"Your *career*?" asked Connie, raising an eyebrow. "I thought the whole point of you coming to Camp Rock was to have fun and hang out with other kids who love music like you do."

"Of course it is," said Mitchie. "But it also helps to build a fan base, and Ginger said the first thing I need to do is refine my image. And I can't do that in the kitchen."

Mitchie hung her apron on the pantry door, checked her reflection in the stainless steel of the walk-in refrigerator, and started for the door.

"Ginger says 'your image'?" Connie repeated, not believing her ears. She rolled her eyes. "You know, you're starting to sound an awful lot like Tess."

Hearing that, Mitchie stopped in her tracks at the door. She turned. "I'll be here extra-early to help with dinner," she said. "I promise."

"Fine." Connie sighed. "Let me know how the YouToo video of the concert turned out."

Mitchie laughed. "You*Tube*," she said, correcting her mother.

Her mother laughed, too. "Whatever!" Connie said, throwing up her hands. "You handle that, and I'll stick to the chili."

"Sounds good," Mitchie said. Smiling, she headed off to find Shane.

Shane already had the video of the concert playing on his iPhone when Mitchie knocked on his cabin door. She could hear herself and Shane singing the refrain of the song through the screen windows.

"Who is it?" Shane called.

Mitchie cracked open the door. "Yours truly," she sang out.

"Ah. Just who I wanted to see," said Shane. "Come on in."

She flopped down in a chair. "Is that the video?" she asked.

"Yep," he said, handing her the phone. "Whoever smuggled in a camera got some pretty decent footage."

Mitchie watched the clip on the small

screen. She nodded her head along to the beat and smiled when the cameras came in for a close-up of Shane. But she frowned when they did the same to her.

"What's wrong?" Shane asked, noticing her frown. He took the phone out of her hand and looked at the screen.

"They didn't get my best angle," said Mitchie. "I look fat from that side, and my hair is totally flat."

Shane's eyes grew large. "Fat?" he repeated in disbelief. "Mitchie, you know you are *not* fat. And your hair looked great."

Mitchie pouted a little, and Shane rolled his eyes. "Please tell me you're not going to become one of those divas," he said.

Mitchie flinched at his use of the word "diva." It reminded her of what her mother had just said.

"I am not a diva!" she protested.

"Well, you will be if you keep talking like that," Shane replied. "Now, if I give this back, will you promise to watch how great you were?"

Mitchie blushed and smiled. "Yes," she promised. She realized how silly she sounded.

"Okay," Shane said and handed the phone back to her. He pressed PLAY again and watched over her shoulder.

"We nailed that note!" Mitchie exclaimed when the video reached a particularly difficult part of the song.

"Now that's more like it." Shane grinned.

CHAPTER EIGHT

Wads of crumpled-up paper were flying around the Vibe Cabin, which could mean only one thing: Ella's weekly care package from her mom had arrived. Each week, Ella's mother shipped a box full of candy, CDs, makeup, nail polish, and—best of all—the latest copy of all the entertainment magazines, including Ella's favorite, *Celeb Beat*.

With Tess, Peggy, and Lorraine standing

over her shoulders, Ella ripped through the new package until she got to the magazine at the bottom. She pulled it out of the packing peanuts, but it was immediately snatched from her hands by Tess.

Connect Three was on the cover, but Tess wasn't concerned with that. She flipped furiously through the glossy pages until she found the article on the School Rocks concert.

"Oooh!" squealed Lorraine when Tess found it. "There's a photo of you!"

Sure enough, Lorraine pointed to a picture of Tess and her mother singing onstage as red balloons descended around them.

"That's a great picture, Tess," offered Peggy.

"I know, right?" Tess replied excitedly.

She started to read the article out loud: "'School Rocks met Camp Rock last week when stars aligned to raise money for after-school music programs at a special concert.'"

"Whoo!" Ella and Lorraine clapped and cheered as Tess read on.

"'The lineup included pop sensation and Camp Rock camper-turned-instructor Shane Gray, singing . . . blah blah blah,'" said Tess, skipping ahead. "'Concert organizers brought out Tess Tyler to perform with her mother, pop star and Blush Cosmetics spokesperson T.J. Tyler, when—'"

Suddenly, Tess stopped short. "Never mind," she said, tossing the magazine on her bed. "It's just a stupid little article. It doesn't really say anything."

"What do you mean? You have your name in *Celeb Beat*!" Peggy said, picking up the magazine. "'Concert organizers brought out Tess Tyler,'" Peggy started reading again, "'to perform with her mother, pop star and Blush Cosmetics spokesperson T.J. Tyler, when . . .' Oh," Peggy said.

"When *what*?" Ella asked, taking the magazine from Peggy's hands.

"'When T.J. insisted she wouldn't perform without her daughter,'" shot Tess before Ella had a chance to read it herself. "Okay? There it is in black and white. My mom made them invite me to sing with her."

"I think that's sweet," Lorraine observed. "Your mom obviously loves you a lot if she jeopardized an opportunity like this to make sure she got to sing with you."

Ella and Peggy nodded along.

But Tess was fuming. That may have been true, but. . . . "How did *Celeb Beat* know?" She glared at the page.

"They do have reporters," Peggy pointed out.

"But the concert organizers *promised* my mom they wouldn't tell a soul," Tess said. "It was in their contract. There was no way they would have told."

"Unless," Lorraine said shrewdly, "the magazine had a mole."

"Like the animal that lives in the

ground?" Ella asked, confused.

Peggy rolled her eyes. She adored her cabinmate, but she wasn't always the brightest star in the sky. "No, like a secret inside source," she explained. "A spy."

Tess hadn't really been listening. The mention of a mole had sparked something. "That's it," she said, narrowing her eyes. The day Caitlyn found her crying outside the rehearsal cabin—hadn't she mentioned that her mom only agreed to perform if Tess sang? "And I bet I know who it is."

While Tess was fuming, Mitchie was floating on air. After Shane had made her watch the video again, she had to admit it rocked. To celebrate, she was heading to B-Note for some ice cream.

"Hey," Mitchie said, walking in and spotting Lola, Caitlyn, Barron, and Sander all huddled around a magazine. "What are you guys reading?"

There was a scramble, and Barron stuffed the magazine under his seat.

"What are you talking about?" Caitlyn asked.

"We're not reading anything," Lola said.

"The dictionary!" Sander blurted. Caitlyn shot him a sideways glance.

"You're reading the dictionary?" Mitchie asked. That seemed a rather odd choice for summer reading.

"Yep," said Barron. "Just looking up some words for the new rap we're working on. Wanted to see what rhymes with . . ."

". . . summer," Sander said, nodding.

"How about 'bummer'?" Mitchie offered. "Which is what you all are. A major bummer. I know you're not reading the dictionary. What magazine is it?"

Caitlyn and Lola looked at each other.

"*Celeb Beat*," Caitlyn finally answered.

"Oh!" Mitchie cried. "Can I see it? Is there something on the concert?"

Again, Caitlyn and Lola exchanged worried glances.

"Yeah," Lola said warily. "There's something on the concert."

But no one moved to show Mitchie the magazine.

"So . . . can I see it?" she asked. "Why are you guys acting so weird?"

Caitlyn sighed. "The article's not the most . . . flattering. Barron," she said, and he produced the copy of *Celeb Beat* from under his seat and handed it to Mitchie.

Mitchie flipped through the pages until she got to the article on the concert. SCHOOL ROCKS CAMP ROCK, the headline screamed across the page. There was a photo of T.J. and Tess, and another smaller one of Mitchie and Shane.

"I don't think the pictures are so bad," Mitchie observed. "I mean, I know I'm not the *most* photogenic person in the world—"

"Read the article," Caitlyn said.

Nervously, Mitchie read: "'Newcomer Mitchie Torres had no trouble adjusting to the bright lights. On the contrary, she was quite the pop princess. The camp chef's daughter demanded her own hair and makeup team and refused to drink anything but Evian water. She may have been Shane Gray's backup, but sources tell *Celeb Beat* that Torres was the one calling the shots.'"

Mitchie was horrified. "What are they talking about?" she said, her mouth dropping open in astonishment. "*They* gave me a hair and makeup team! I didn't ask for one. And I said I didn't care what kind of water I had."

She looked from Caitlyn and Lola to Sander and Barron. They shrugged. Mitchie kept reading: "'Several campers commented on Torres's divalike behavior. "Mitchie's cool, but I guess you could say this concert's kind of gone to her head," one source told *Celeb Beat*. "I'm not sure why only Mitchie gets to perform," said another camper, who requested anonymity. "She hasn't even won a jam yet." ' "

Once again, Mitchie looked at her friends' faces, wondering if any of them were the magazine's "anonymous sources." Tears filled her eyes.

"I didn't know it had gone to my head," she said quietly, the tears falling down her cheeks and landing on the glossy pages of the magazine.

"You know how those things are," Lola said, nodding at the magazine clutched in Mitchie's hands. "They exaggerate everything."

"People get quoted out of context," added Caitlyn, nodding.

Mitchie sniffled. "Yeah, sure," she said, dropping the magazine to the floor as she stood to go. She suddenly felt like being alone. The wave of excitement she'd been riding had come crashing down, leaving her drained.

"I'll catch you guys later," Mitchie said, heading to her cabin.

Once Mitchie was gone, Caitlyn turned to her friends. "Okay," Caitlyn said urgently. "Who talked to the magazine? I know that Mitchie got wrapped up in the spotlight, but that's no reason to go to the press."

"I didn't!" Lola said, wide-eyed.

"Not us," insisted Barron and Sander.

"That's just weird," Caitlyn mused. "Because *someone* was talking, and *Celeb Beat* was listening."

CHAPTER NINE

"Look, Brown, we have a mole. A very well-informed mole. It's *your* job to find out who it is before he—or she—does any more damage," Tess demanded.

Shane, Mitchie, Caitlyn, and Dee were in Brown's office. At first, everyone started talking over each other. But, as usual, Tess had managed to make herself heard.

"It's true, Uncle Brown," Shane said. "How

else would *Celeb Beat* find out all this inside information?"

"But who would it be?" Caitlyn asked.

"I thought it might be you," Tess said, nodding in Caitlyn's direction. "Until I read the rest of the article. You wouldn't say those things about Mitchie."

"Thanks for the vote of confidence," said Caitlyn. "But the only people I was talking to were from camp."

"Me, too," Shane said. "Except for my publicist, my manager, and my agent. And Nate and Jason, of course."

"How do we know it wasn't one of them?" Tess asked. She was getting more and more worked up. "What if Nate and Jason planted the information with a reporter so you and Connect Three would get more press?"

"Enough!" Brown interjected. "I understand this is frustrating . . . and frankly, I'm surprised *Celeb Beat* went ahead and printed those unauthorized photos and story in the first place."

"Maybe . . ." Tess started.

"*But*," Brown finished, cutting off Tess, "I will handle it."

"Handle it how?" she scoffed. "By sending out a press release?"

"I said I'll handle it, Tess," Brown said firmly. "In the meantime, continue as you would." His message delivered, he ordered them out of his office.

"'Continue as you would,'" Mitchie mimicked, rolling her eyes. "Like that's gonna be easy, knowing that *Celeb Beat* has a journalist embedded here. I feel like someone's watching my every move!"

"And waiting to criticize it," Tess pointed out as she, Mitchie, Caitlyn, and Shane walked down the front-porch steps.

Inside, Brown turned to his music director. "You know, Dee," he said, "this is the part of rock 'n' roll that I never liked."

"What's that?" Dee asked.

"All the hoopla and the celebrity that gets blown out of proportion—and the negative press. Why do we always want to build our rock stars up just to tear them down?"

Dee sighed. "Good question."

"I guess I was just hoping that at camp, at least, these kids wouldn't have to deal with all that."

"Maybe it's better that they learn about it sooner rather than later," Dee observed, trying to put a positive spin on it.

It was Brown's turn to sigh. "Maybe," he said. "But now we have a mole to find."

Knowing that *Celeb Beat* had its eyes and ears trained on them had everyone at Camp Rock on edge. At the Mess Hall of Fame, campers spoke to each other in hushed whispers. In the B-Note canteen, people talked about "safe" things, such as the weather or the upcoming Bonfire Jamboree.

And in classes, everyone was superfocused. If a reporter really *was* at Camp Rock, he—or she—would be getting nothing but stories about dedicated, well-behaved campers.

Mitchie, however, still hadn't gotten over the sting of her fellow campers talking about her. Was it true what they said? she wondered. Had she been acting like a diva? She hadn't meant to. People were just offering her things and telling her ways to look good. When you were treated like rock royalty, it sure was easy to act like it! She couldn't help but sort of get why Tess was the way she was. But still—that wasn't her. She hated the idea of others getting that impression.

Since reading the article, Mitchie had decided laying low was the best option. So she had been staying pretty quiet. Now, in songwriting class, she broke the silence with Lola and Caitlyn.

"Hey, guys," Mitchie said suddenly, as the three girls were puzzling over a word that rhymed with "bonfire" for the jamboree.

Lola and Caitlyn looked up from their notepads.

"I'm sorry," Mitchie said, "if I was acting kind of spoiled before the concert . . . and during the concert . . . and after the concert. I just wasn't used to all the attention."

Caitlyn smiled. "We know," she said.

"Water under the bridge," assured Lola.

Mitchie smiled, realizing how good the friends she had made this summer at Camp Rock really were. "Thanks, you guys," she said, breathing a huge sigh of relief.

"Just promise us you and Tess won't start your own divas tour," Caitlyn joked.

Mitchie laughed. "Cross my heart," she said, using her finger to cross her chest. The girls fell into a comfortable silence. Even though she had apologized, something was still weighing on Mitchie. She finally spoke up. "I just keep wondering if people really said those things about me."

Lola shrugged. "Maybe they did, maybe they didn't," she said. "If they did, it was probably because they were a little jealous that you got to perform at a really cool concert. Either way, you can't worry about it."

Just then, Tess wandered up. Ella and Lorraine were, for once, not trailing behind her. "What are you talking about?" she asked.

"We're just talking about the article," answered Caitlyn.

"And how *not* fun it is to be put under a microscope," Mitchie added.

They all were expecting Tess to make some flippant remark, but instead she grew serious. "It's not easy being famous," she said. "People write things about you that aren't true . . . and some things that are true but that are nobody's business. My mom's stopped reading magazines altogether."

"Really?" Lola asked, surprised by both Tess's honesty and the idea that T.J. Tyler *didn't* read about herself.

Just then Mac walked up, catching the tail end of the conversation.

"What's up?" he asked.

"We're just talking about that article in *Celeb Beat*," Mitchie answered this time.

"Ya know," Caitlyn said, thinking about it, "if I ever get my hands on the reporter who made up that story . . ." She narrowed her eyes and made a motion with her hands like she was wringing someone's neck.

"Oh. Well . . . I better get back to my boys," Mac said, nodding toward Colby and Andy.

"Liar!" Caitlyn suddenly exclaimed.

Mac's face turned ashen. "Huh?" he asked.

"Liar," Caitlyn repeated. "It rhymes with 'bonfire.' Can we use that for the next verse?"

She had turned her attention back to the lyrics on the notebook in front of her.

"Oh, right." Mac chuckled. "That would work. See y'all later," he said nervously and quickly headed over to the table where Colby and Andy were sitting.

Shrugging at his speedy retreat, Caitlyn, Mitchie, and Lola got back to work.

"**W**here did that thing go?" asked a confounded Colby. He was on his knees, searching under the dusty bunk beds in his cabin for his last guitar pick. He should have known to bring more than one box to Camp Rock!

"I thought I dropped it between the bed and the wall," he was muttering when Mac walked in.

All Mac could see was Colby's rear end sticking out from under a cot. "Hey, roomie," he said.

Colby bumped his head as he withdrew from under the bed. "Ow!" he cried, rubbing his head as he stood up from the floor. "Have you seen my tortoise-shell guitar pick?" he asked.

"Nope," Mac said, grabbing a fresh shirt from his trunk. Dance practice had left him sweaty. "Sorry. But you can borrow one of mine if you want."

"Thanks, man. Are you sure?" Colby asked.

"Yeah. Of course," replied Mac, sliding an old concert T-shirt over his head. "They're in my trunk. Help yourself. Gotta run."

Without thinking about what he'd just done, Mac dashed out of the cabin. He was supposed to meet Caitlyn down at B-Note for a producing lesson in five minutes and didn't want to be late.

Colby pried open the lid of Mac's trunk. Inside, next to the box of guitar picks, was a tape recorder. The kind reporters used.

"Hmm," Colby said to himself, picking up the minirecorder. He pressed PLAY.

Suddenly, Colby heard the voice of a girl he recognized as Ashley speak: "I'm not sure why only Mitchie gets to perform. She hasn't even won a jam yet."

It was the quote from the magazine article! Only Ashley didn't sound ticked off or

103

jealous the way the article made it seem, just genuinely uncertain.

Colby gasped. It took him a second to register what he was hearing. Then he noticed another thing in Mac's trunk—a reporter's spiral notebook, small and skinny and lined. Colby leaned down to read the writing on the front page. In Mac's familiar handwriting it read, "T.J. Tyler demanded that Tess perform."

Colby straightened up. He and Mac had become pretty tight since they'd arrived at camp. As a new kid like him, and a Southern guy to boot, Mac knew what it was like to feel out of place sometimes at Camp Rock, surrounded by kids who'd been there since the first session and who grew up in places like Los Angeles and New York.

But it had all been a lie. *Mac* was the undercover reporter! Maybe, Colby thought, I don't know my cabinmate as well as I thought I did.

CHAPTER TEN

After making his discovery, Colby had decided there was only one thing he could do—go to Brown's office and tell him about what he had found in Mac's trunk. Colby didn't want to believe his friend was secretly covering Camp Rock for *Celeb Beat* magazine, but he had to admit the evidence was overwhelming.

"Now, you're sure?" Brown asked once

Colby had stated his case. This was not good—not good at all.

"I'm sure," Colby assured Brown. "The recorder and notebook were right there in his trunk next to the guitar picks."

Brown shook his head in disappointment. "Well, I'll just have to see what Mac says for himself. Thank you, Colby. You did the right thing by telling me. I know it's hard when a friend hasn't been truthful with you."

Colby nodded gloomily and headed to his guitar class.

Picking up one of the walkie-talkies Dee had gotten them so they could communicate across camp, Brown called her up.

"Dee?" he said into the walkie-talkie. It crackled.

"Yes, Brown. Over." Dee's voice came through the yellow walkie-talkie.

"You don't have to say 'over,' Dee. I can hear you just fine."

"Okay. Over. Oops! Sorry." Dee apologized.

Brown rolled his eyes good-naturedly. "Have you seen Mac this afternoon?" he asked her.

"Sure have. He's at the lake," Dee said cheerfully. "He's out in a canoe at the moment with Caitlyn Gellar. Do you need him for something?"

"Could you please ask him to come to my office immediately?" said Brown. "It's important."

"Sure thing," said Dee. "Over and out."

The walkie-talkie went silent, and Brown sighed. If there was one thing he hated about being camp director, it was having to discipline campers. But if there was one thing he couldn't have at Camp Rock, it was reporters bothering the campers and counselors.

"You wanted to see me?" Mac said as he stood in the doorway of Brown's office a few minutes later. His face was pale despite the fact that he'd been out in the sun. Getting

107

called into the director's office could mean nothing good.

"Yes, Mac. Come in, please," Brown said, walking around to sit on the edge of his desk.

Mac anxiously took a seat in front of the director.

Brown took a deep breath. "Mac, something has recently come to my attention concerning the incident with the *Celeb Beat* article." He watched for Mac's reaction. "But before I jump to conclusions, I'd like to see if there's anything you'd like to tell me first."

Mac's face fell. His mind raced. Suddenly he remembered letting Colby get the guitar picks from his trunk. That was where he kept his tape recorder for his reporting! Colby must have told Brown Mac's secret. And from the look on Brown's face, he was seriously disappointed. Mac felt a wave of guilt wash over him. He had never meant for people to get hurt. . . .

"I guess there is something I should tell

you," Mac said softly. He fidgeted as he tried to decide where to begin. "When I came to Camp Rock, it wasn't necessarily because I wanted to be a rock star—or even a musician." He paused. "It was because I wanted to be a rock journalist."

Brown nodded slowly, waiting to hear Mac's story.

Mac continued. "*Celeb Beat* gave me an internship. They loved the idea that I could report from inside camp, getting the campers' perspective and all."

"So you wrote the article on the School Rocks concert?" Brown asked.

Mac shook his head. "No, I just sent the editor my notes and some quotes. She wrote the article."

Brown was silent as he decided what to do.

"Are you gonna kick me out?" Mac asked nervously.

"No, mate," Brown said solemnly. "I haven't kicked a camper out yet, and I'm not going to start now. Rock reporters are part of the music industry, and I am impressed by your drive. I understand how it could be hard to pass up such an opportunity. But I hope *you* understand that I can't allow you to report on Camp Rock. I want campers to feel this is a place where they can explore their musical talents and be themselves without being judged. It can't be that way if they're afraid of ending up in *Celeb Beat* magazine."

Mac nodded. He understood. After all the negative fallout from the article, he was beginning to wonder if reporting for *Celeb Beat* was what he really wanted to do anyway.

"So," Brown continued, "I'm going to let you stay on two conditions. One, you won't report on us for *Celeb Beat* anymore."

Mac nodded.

"Two, you'll apologize to the whole camp at the Bonfire Jamboree tonight."

Mac gulped but nodded again. "Deal," he said, standing to shake Brown's hand. "I'm sorry for any trouble I caused, Brown."

Brown slapped Mac on the shoulder. "I know you are. I remember when my friend Cameron toured with us as a reporter for *Rolling Stone*. Boy, some of the stuff he wrote really ticked off my band!" Brown chuckled. "We forgave him, though. We knew there was always truth in what he wrote, and we knew he covered music because he loved it as much as we did."

"Thanks, Brown. I just hope my friends will forgive me."

Brown thought about this as he walked Mac to the door. "I bet they will," he said. "You just think about what you want to say tonight at the bonfire. Remember, it's all in the presentation.

Down by the lake, the bonfire was going strong. The reflection of its orange flames danced on the water behind the fire pit. The campers were excited. They'd been working on camp songs all week. That was the theme—regular summer camp songs with a rock twist. Connie had even set up a s'mores table so the campers could roast marshmallows and build their own gooey, chocolatey graham cracker sandwiches.

Now campers and counselors sat in a semicircle around the bonfire, waiting for Brown and Dee. Some of their suspicion about the *Celeb Beat* undercover reporter had worn off, and they were talking excitedly again.

Mac, however, was silent. He knew in a matter of minutes he'd have to tell everyone that he was the one who'd given *Celeb Beat* their information. He was sure Tess and Mitchie would be furious. Not to mention Shane. He *knew* Colby was angry. And then there was Caitlyn. He was worried about her reaction the most.

Mac's silence hadn't gone unnoticed by Caitlyn. They were sitting next to each other on a log by the fire. Mitchie and Shane were next to them, followed by Lola, Peggy, Ella, Lorraine, and Tess. Everyone was there. Except for Colby. He'd chosen to sit on the other side of the fire.

"Are you okay?" Caitlyn asked, eyeing Mac. "You're being really . . . quiet."

"Yeah," Mac said. "I'm okay." But, in truth, his stomach was in knots and his palms were sweaty. He was not looking forward to this.

"Okay," Caitlyn said, jumping up. "I'm gonna make a s'more. Anyone with me?"

"Ooh! Me," Mitchie said, also jumping up.

"You don't have a personal assistant to make one for you?" Shane joked.

"Ha-ha," Mitchie laughed sarcastically. "Don't you know my diva days are behind me?"

"Does that mean you've decided to step down from the pop princess throne?" Caitlyn joked.

"I think I like being a commoner better,"

replied Mitchie. Laughing, Mitchie and Caitlyn headed for the marshmallows. As they did, Brown walked up to Mac.

"You ready?" Brown asked him.

Mac sighed heavily and stood up. "Ready as I'll ever be."

Colby watched Mac as he walked to stand in front of the fire, before the campers. Shane was also watching, wondering what Mac was up to.

Brown stood next to Mac and waited for the campers to take their seats and get quiet. Finally, the only noise was that of the crickets and a few motorboats on the lake.

"Before we start the traditional jamboree," Brown said, "Mac would like to share something with all of us. I hope you'll hear him out."

Brown went to sit next to Dee. Mac cleared his throat. His heart felt like it was going to jump out of his chest.

"Hey, y'all," Mac started. Everyone stared

at him, confused. This was unusual. "I know some of you were upset with the recent article in *Celeb Beat* about the School Rocks concert. It wasn't the most flattering—or even accurate—article. And some of you have been concerned that the magazine had an undercover reporter here at Camp Rock."

Mac took a deep breath and looked at Caitlyn as he made his confession. "That reporter was actually me."

Campers gasped and everyone started whispering excitedly. There had been a mole after all! Caitlyn's jaw dropped. Mitchie was confused, and Shane was angry. Colby's face was impassive.

Now that the initial confession was out, the rest of the words came easier. "I came to Camp Rock to report for *Celeb Beat* from the inside," Mac said, speaking up to be heard over the commotion. "I want—or wanted—to be a rock journalist. But I didn't anticipate how it would make people feel to have their friend reporting on them. I'm sorry if I hurt your feelings by writing about you behind your backs."

A couple campers, including Barron and Sander, started booing from the crowd. But Brown quickly came to stand next to Mac.

"All right now," Brown said to the crowd. "Mac has said he's sorry and assured me that he has done the last of his reporting as a Camp Rock correspondent." Mac nodded heartily in confirmation. "I think we can chalk this up to another lesson learned about the business of rock and roll and let bygones be bygones. Now, on with the jamboree!"

Two campers took Mac and Brown's spot in front of the bonfire. Giggling, they proceeded with their new camp song about fishing.

Mac headed back to where he'd been sitting. Tess met him halfway, trailed by Ella and Lorraine. "So, you're the mole?" Tess said, glaring at Mac.

Mac hung his head. "I *was* the mole. Like

Brown said, I've reported my last story from Camp Rock. I'm sorry, Tess."

"Well," Ella said, seeing how sorry Mac really was and trying to look on the bright side, "if it weren't for you, there might not have been *any* article in *Celeb Beat* about Tess. You know what they say, 'any press is good press.'"

Tess shrugged. "The pictures were good. And my mom said *Teen Weekly* magazine has already called her to do a mother-daughter interview with us. So I guess I owe you that. . . ."

Mac brightened at that news. Maybe there was a chance for forgiveness after all. But Shane was storming up, and he did not look very sympathetic.

"What were you thinking, Mac?" Shane asked angrily. "You really hurt Mitchie's feelings with all that stuff you wrote."

Mitchie was behind Shane. "Shane," she said, putting her hand gently on his shoulder.

"It's okay. It did hurt my feelings, but what Mac reported was true. I *did* get carried away with all the attention and the royal treatment. I *was* being a diva. You even said so yourself."

"I was joking," Shane argued. "And I didn't publish it for the whole world to read."

"Yeah." Mitchie shrugged. "But like Tess said the other day, that's just the other side of being famous. It's part of the bargain. You, of all people, should know that. No one is really like they're portrayed in the magazines. You can't judge a CD by its cover—or a person by his or her press."

Grudgingly, Shane stepped back. He shoved his hands deep in his jean pockets. "You're right," he said. "I just never thought 'the press' would be one of my friends."

Mac gulped. "Are we?" he asked with a distressed look on his face. "Still friends, I mean. If I promise never to write another story about you ever again?"

Mitchie answered for them all.

"Yes," she said. "Of course. Camp Rockers stick together."

Mac looked relieved. He threw his arms around Mitchie and then a surprised Shane.

But there were two Camp Rockers he wasn't sure would still call him a friend— Colby and Caitlyn. And they were talking together just beyond the light of the bonfire.

"Excuse me," Mac said. "I think there are a couple more people I still have to personally apologize to."

Mitchie and Shane nodded, and Mac walked shyly up to Caitlyn and Colby.

"Hi," he said sheepishly.

"Hi," they answered in unison.

"You lied to me," Colby said. "You lied to all of us."

"I know," said Mac. "I did, and I'm sorry."

"How are we supposed to ever trust you again?" asked Caitlyn.

Mac sighed. "I don't know," he said. "All I

can ask is that you try," he said. "And if I lie to you again, I give you permission to hang me from my toes by the flagpole."

Caitlyn and Colby couldn't stifle their laughter. "All right," said Caitlyn, "but I'm holding you to that."

"Me, too," Colby said, and the three of them walked back toward the bonfire and their other friends, chuckling at the thought of a helpless Mac hanging upside down from the flagpole.

When they were seated, Brown came up and squatted down next to Mac. "I've been thinking, Mac, and I have one more condition in order for you to stay at Camp Rock," he said.

"Okay," Mac replied nervously.

"You'll promise to write a Camp Rock newsletter," said Brown.

Mac smiled. "Actually, I think I've decided to leave journalism behind. I've found a new passion at Camp Rock."

"What's that?" asked Brown.

"Music producing." Mac grinned and looked at Caitlyn. "I have a good teacher."

Caitlyn blushed.

"But a newsletter would help us all keep in touch after camp," Mitchie offered.

"In that case," Mac said, as campers sang a song about Camp Rock in front of the bonfire, "I'll do it."

He was sure that was going to be one story worth writing.

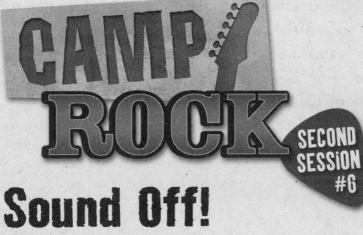

Sound Off!

By James Ponti

Based on "Camp Rock," Written by Karin Gist & Regina Hicks and Julie Brown & Paul Brown

Mitchie Torres was not a morning person. It didn't matter if she was at home during the school year or at Camp Rock in the summer, her goal was to get up at the last possible moment. The fact that musicians usually performed at night and slept late the following morning was part of the appeal of a life in rock and roll. But this morning the piercing sound of an alarm clock was making sleep all but impossible.

At least it was for Mitchie.

On the other side of the cabin, her best friend, Caitlyn Gellar, was sleeping like a baby, completely unaffected by the alarm's buzz.

Mitchie attempted to block out the sound by wrapping a pillow around her head. When that didn't work, she tried a blanket. Out of frustration, she chucked the pillow across the room and hit Caitlyn right in the head. If she was going to suffer, she at least wanted to suffer with company.

But Caitlyn just took a swat at it as if it were a mosquito and rolled over, all without waking up.

Finally, brushing her brown bangs out of

her eyes, Mitchie got up and walked over to Caitlyn's nightstand. As loudly as she could, she turned off the alarm.

"Wake up!" Mitchie cried, shaking her friend by the shoulder. "It's the least you can do considering it's *your* alarm clock going off."

"What time is it?" Caitlyn asked, half-speaking, half-yawning.

"Six!" Mitchie exclaimed. "In the morning!"

It took a moment for this to sink in, but when it did, Caitlyn panicked. "It's not six," she stammered as her eyes finally focused on her clock. "It's 6:03. Do you know what that means? Today is Sound Off!"